Wrongway
Applebaum

Wrongway

...eye on the ball Stan...

pictures by
Margot Apple

Applebaum

by
Marjorie Lewis

Coward-McCann Inc.   New York

Second printing

Library of Congress Cataloging in Publication Data
Lewis, Marjorie
Wrongway Applebaum
Summary: Always a little slow and awkward,
Applebaum dreams of being on the baseball team and
impressing everyone with his spectacular playing.
[1. Baseball—Fiction. 2. Schools—Fiction]
I. Apple, Margot, ill. II. Title
PZ7.L58727Wr   1984   [Fic]   84-3242
ISBN 0-698-20610-X

For Danny, who
runs the right way

MY THANKS TO

Phil, who remembered his coaching days,

and David and Jim, who remembered their playing days,

and Gary Nusbaum and his father Jack, for checking
on the facts with the Major League umpires,

and Little League headquarters who took time
to explain the rules to me,

and Skip Bertman, whose memories and book,
Coaching Youth League Baseball, were invaluable,

and Harriet Lyons who, as always,
was there when I needed her.

Wrongway Applebaum

1

Spring came just when the fifth grade had finished fractions and Indians and was beginning decimals and Africa. Spring was also the beginning of the baseball season. There was an exhibit of books about baseball in the library and the fifth grade chose up sides and played baseball during recess. Applebaum was always the last one to be picked for a team.

Applebaum's first name was Stanley, but nobody called him Stanley except his teachers. From the time he had started school, everyone in his class had called him "Applebaum." Applebaum's mother and father and relatives called him "Stanley," of course, except when he and his father played baseball. Then his father called him "Stan" as if that were a tougher name that might belong to a future baseball star. Now that it was spring and stayed light later in the evenings, Applebaum's father had him out in the yard after dinner throwing, batting, and catching. Actually, his father threw and Applebaum tried his best to bat and catch. But even with the glove his father had given him as a birthday present, Applebaum couldn't catch. And when the ball his father threw came toward the bat, Applebaum couldn't connect. Ever. Applebaum's father showed him the way to stand, the way to clutch the bat, and the way to follow the ball to make the catch. He showed Applebaum what to do again and again. "Now, Stan," he would say, "keep your elbows up." And, "Now, Stan, keep your eye on the ball. ON THE BALL! STAN!" Again and again Applebaum missed the ball with the bat or with the glove. And off into the neighbor's yard the ball would go—right past him, until neither he nor his father could see enough in the gathering darkness to find it.

Everyone in Applebaum's family cared about baseball. Applebaum's grandmother knew everything about every player and every team, even players and teams from a long, long time ago. The television set that Applebaum and his mother and father had given her for her birthday a few years ago was turned on all day during baseball season in the knitting store she owned. She and her customers would knit sweaters and watch ball games and talk baseball together. Applebaum's mother had played softball when she was a girl and Applebaum had seen pictures of her up at bat with long braids, and a baseball cap shading her eyes as she stood at the plate. Applebaum's father had played baseball in high school (where he had made the all-county, all-star team) and then in college. Applebaum knew his father dreamed of the day his son would be a star baseball player. In fact, Applebaum had the same dream. He dreamed of hitting the winning run in an important game and being carried on the shoulders of the crowd; he dreamed of cheers from the sidelines—

"RAH! RAH! STAN!" the crowd would yell; he dreamed of handshakes and good-natured backslapping by the members of his own team. And then, dreamed Applebaum, they would invite him to their birthday parties, or, best of all, to go to the movies and have a hamburger or something after the show. "That isn't much too much to ask," thought Applebaum as he dreamed his dreams.

Actually, Applebaum was afraid. He was uncomfortable with the other kids; he couldn't think of things to say to them. He was afraid they would laugh at him. When he played baseball, he was afraid of getting hit with a fastball and he closed his eyes when the ball was pitched to him, so he couldn't see when to hit it.

Applebaum couldn't remember the rules of *any* game, just as he couldn't remember other things most people thought were important, like what his homework assignment was, the directions for taking a test, or where he had left his jacket. Most of all, Applebaum found it hard to remember left and right and clockwise and

counterclockwise. He had a terrible time learning to read and spell, but he was getting better as he grew older. Fifth grade was easier than first grade had been. Applebaum had learned that if he could just concentrate until he got his bearings and then do what he had to do, things usually came out pretty well. But he had to think things out first and rehearse them in his mind before he did them.

The other kids left Applebaum pretty much to himself. Nobody teased him, but, then, nobody talked to him much about anything. Only Applebaum's family thought he had any possibilities. Applebaum's mother helped him with his homework, reminded him of things he had to remember, and tacked up his papers and stuff on the walls of the kitchen when he had done something well. But Applebaum knew that he still had a long way to go.

When some of the fifth graders—Ernie, Frankie, Alfred, Cynthia, Eleanor, and Edward—decided to try to join the local school baseball league and have a real fifth grade team, they had no thought at all of including Applebaum. But Applebaum knew that being part of that team was what he wanted most of all.

2

All the fifth grades from the elementary schools in the area that belonged to the league played each other. The winning fifth grade team each year had a barbecue to celebrate. Applebaum knew that sometimes the losers had a barbecue too, just to make themselves feel better, but he thought that the winners' barbecue was probably a happier one.

Besides the barbecue, the players on the winning team got trophies that looked like Oscars, only with baseball hats on and bats in their hands. Applebaum had just the right space on his bookshelves for a trophy. He knew that if he ever won one, he would keep it forever to show his own children. It would be the first one, he said to himself. And the other trophies would get bigger and more important as the years went by. Maybe the time would come when his father would have to build a room for his trophies, dreamed Applebaum. Everyone had to start somewhere, after all.

Applebaum also knew that the team members' parents, and sisters, and brothers, and teachers, and—sometimes—aunts and uncles and grandparents and friends came to watch them play and to cheer their favorite team to victory. In his dream, Applebaum could see his parents smiling and cheering as he hit the winning run. Especially his father. When he was a star, Applebaum decided, he would have STAN, or maybe even BIG STAN, embroidered on the front of a gorgeous satin zipper jacket.

To join the league, the fifth grade had to have a coach who would help them win and a sponsor who would give them T-shirts with the team name on the front and the sponsor's name on the back and treat them to ice cream when they won a game, or even if they didn't. Applebaum knew that Ernie and his friends were going to look for a sponsor on Saturday morning. They were going to go from store to store in the village and ask in each store if the owner would like to be their sponsor. Applebaum decided that the time had come to make his move. He told himself that maybe they wouldn't laugh at him if he asked to go along. He told himself that he wasn't getting any younger—it might be his last chance to be part of a team and he should do his darndest to get in at the ground floor while things were still in the planning stage.

When Applebaum finally got his courage up enough to ask if he could go with Ernie and the others on Saturday morning, they were too surprised to say no. "I didn't know you wanted to play baseball, Applebaum," said Ernie.

"I didn't know you *could* play baseball," said Frankie.

Everybody else stood around not saying anything. There was silence for a long time. Finally Ernie said he supposed it would be OK. Then he told Applebaum where they were going to meet and what time.

"I'll be there," said Applebaum, and walked away.

When he had gone, Alfred said, "I can't believe it. Applebaum has never, ever, in all the years I've known him—since kindergarten—said a word to me."

Eleanor said, "It doesn't hurt to be nice."

"Applebaum is trying very hard to learn his fifth grade work," said Cynthia, "and maybe he's ready to make some friends now he's feeling better about himself."

Ernie said that Applebaum had given him half a sandwich one day when he had forgotten his lunch and maybe Applebaum wasn't so bad once you got to know him. Edward said that he'd do his best to be nice, but it would be hard to be friends with someone who was such a jerk.

3

It was a beautiful Saturday morning. Applebaum tagged along as Ernie and his friends went into one store after another looking for a sponsor. But all the stores already had teams: the bowling alley was sponsoring another fifth grade team; the paint store had a sixth grade team and a fourth grade team too. The deli had another sixth grade team. It certainly seemed as if nobody was interested in sponsoring the fifth grade team from Applebaum's school. Applebaum and the others sat down on the curb to discuss the problem. The others talked about how they would have to find a coach too. Applebaum listened.

"I can't think of anyone to go to next," said Ernie.

Eleanor said that maybe they didn't need a sponsor at all. "We can just be independent," she said.

Frankie said that it would mean no uniforms or anything unless they bought them themselves and that would be expensive. Everyone sat silently looking down at the gutter.

"Uh," said Applebaum. "Uh, I have an idea."

The others had forgotten Applebaum was with them. They turned their heads to look at him.

Then Applebaum said that his grandmother owned Sophie's Place, the local knitting store.

"So what," said Alfred.

"So she knows all about our class. She read about us in the newspaper last year when Ernie taught us all to knit. Well," added Applebaum softly, "almost all of us. And she knows lots about baseball."

Everyone knew that Applebaum had been the only person in the fourth grade who hadn't been able to learn to knit. Applebaum had helped out at the fair, for which everyone had knitted all kinds of things and sold home-baked cookies as well as knitted items, but he had messed things up by giving the wrong change when customers paid for what they bought. When Ernie's class made the front page of the paper and Ernie showed off the almost mile-long muffler he had knitted from scraps of yarn everyone had given him, Applebaum had been absent. His mother had called school and said he had a stomachache, but Ernie thought it was just an excuse because Applebaum was embarrassed to be there among all the happy knitters. It was too bad, Ernie had thought. After all, Applebaum had *tried* to knit.

Frankie said that knitting shops didn't ordinarily do such things as sponsor baseball teams even if the owner's grandson was on the team. Alfred said he wasn't sure he wanted to be sponsored by a knitting store. But Cynthia, who was a good shortstop, said, "Well, we have no choice. We won't be able to play otherwise. I think we should check it out."

Applebaum said that because Ernie was the

most talented knitter among them Ernie should go with him to talk to his grandmother.

When Applebaum and Ernie went inside, Frankie said, "I suppose if she says yes then Applebaum will have to play. And that will mean we'll never win a game."

They could hear the bell tinkle as Applebaum and Ernie closed the door to the shop.

In a few minutes Applebaum and Ernie came outside. Applebaum didn't say anything, but Ernie said, "I have some good news and some bad news." The good news, Ernie told them, was that Sophie wanted to be their sponsor and would supply T-shirts with the team name on the front and her store name on the back. And caps, too. The bad news was that Sophie wanted to be the coach as well as the sponsor.

"No way," said Frankie. "I refuse to be coached by an old lady—especially Applebaum's grandmother!" Then he grumbled, "It's bad enough being sponsored by a knitting shop, for heaven's sake!"

Eleanor, who was the best pitcher in the class,

said that neither being old nor a lady was a problem. "Besides," she said, "we haven't even seen her. We don't know if she *is* very old. The important thing is does Sophie know enough about baseball to coach a team?" Applebaum didn't say a word.

Then Sophie came out of her store and said she had heard of them and their knitting. She didn't look too old. She stood with her arm across Applebaum's shoulders. "I've always wanted a baseball team of my own to sponsor and to coach, only nobody's ever asked me. Now is my chance. The chance of a lifetime. And how wonderful," she added, "to be able to coach my Stanley and his friends." Sophie said that she knew they weren't thrilled about having somebody's grandmother for a coach or a knitting store for a sponsor, but, she said, she'd have her name on the shirts too. "How do I know you guys can play and won't embarrass *me?*" she asked.

Frankie said, "We're pretty good—except for . . . "

Before he could finish, Sophie told them she was willing to take a chance. "Your problem is that you can play but don't know if I can coach. I know I can coach but I don't know if you can

play. It seems to me we have to trust each other."

"I think we ought to talk about it and then take a vote," said Ernie. Then he asked Sophie if she would go back inside while they voted. When they heard the bell tinkle as Sophie closed the door behind her, Frankie said that all the other teams would laugh at them. Cynthia said that maybe they would at first, but they sure would stop when they saw some terrific playing.

"Not all of us are terrific," said Edward, looking at Applebaum.

"It's like she said, we have to trust each other," said Eleanor.

Then Frankie said, "The whole idea stinks!"

Ernie asked Alfred what he thought, but Alfred said he didn't know what he thought. On the one hand they were going to have to be awfully good so people wouldn't laugh at them; on the other hand if Sophie were the kind of coach she said she was, they *would* be that good.

Ernie called for a vote without asking Applebaum anything at all. Cynthia's hand went up first; then Alfred's; then Ernie's; then Eleanor's. Very slowly, Frankie raised his hand. Edward said, "Count me in."

Applebaum raised his hand high and smiled. Then he said, "Uh, we need a captain." The others nodded in agreement. "I nominate Ernie," said Applebaum. Once again they voted, but since nobody else's name was proposed, it was unanimous. Ernie was the captain of the team. His first duty was to go inside and get Sophie.

Very shortly, Ernie and Sophie came out of the store. Sophie had a pencil and a clipboard with a pad on it. She sat down on the curb and wrote down each of their names and telephone numbers. "I know yours, of course," said Sophie, smiling at Applebaum.

Sophie told them she would call the school to find out about borrowing equipment, getting field time for practice, and making contact with the league. Then she stood up, put a sign on her door that said BACK IN FIFTEEN MINUTES, locked up, and took them across the street for ice cream.

While they were eating, Sophie told them that they were fulfilling a secret dream of hers. "Baseball is my hobby," she said. "I watch all the games on my TV at home or on my small set in the store." Then she told them that when she was growing up, she had been a fine hitter but the boys wouldn't let her play with them and there were no girls' teams. "I remember how bad I felt when nobody would let me play. It's very important that any boy *or* girl who wants to play on the team is welcome. Even if they aren't very good," said Sophie, looking at Applebaum, "I think that with the right coaching they'll be valuable to the team." Then Sophie asked Ernie to make an announcement during homeroom period in school on Monday that anyone in the fifth grade who wanted to join the team should show up for practice. She said she would let Ernie know what time they were scheduled to use the field.

4

Monday morning during homeroom time, Ernie made the announcement about the team and told the class that the first practice would be the following Saturday morning. He told them that their coach (who was also their sponsor and the lady who owned the knitting store and Applebaum's grandmother) had said that anyone who wanted to play could join the team. Some of the kids snickered. Only one person said he wanted to play—Richard. Another person said loudly that she wouldn't be caught dead being coached by the knitting lady who was also Applebaum's grandmother. Applebaum didn't say anything. He felt very uncomfortable. Then Ernie told them that Sophie had promised ice cream, T-shirts, and hats, seemed to know what she was doing, and, besides, it was Sophie or nobody. Two more people, Arthur and Philip, said they wanted to play.

Later, when Ernie, Frankie, Edward, and Alfred were discussing the league, they started talking about Applebaum, who was sitting by himself trying to learn his spelling words.

They had all been in school together for almost six years. They knew that Applebaum didn't know his left from his right—he had made Alfred fall off his bicycle once by signaling left and then turning right, cutting Alfred off. "And remember when we used to play circle games in first grade like Duck, Duck, Goose? or the Farmer in the Dell?" asked Frankie. "Applebaum confused the whole class because he never knew which way to go."

Edward recalled that in second grade, when they were all learning to play baseball, Applebaum had accidentally connected for the only hit of his life. Everyone had yelled, "Run home!

Run home!" And Applebaum had done just
that. He had run all the way to his house, in the
front door, and was sitting down to milk and
cookies when Ernie and Alfred arrived to bring
him back.

Also, Applebaum couldn't remember how to
play any position in any game. He was hopeless

during gym periods and frustrated Mr. Antonio, the gym teacher, because he couldn't teach Applebaum how to do anything correctly.

"There's nothing we can do about it," said Ernie. "Applebaum has to be on the team."

"We'll never win a game if he plays," said Frankie.

"We'll never have any games to play if he doesn't," said Alfred.

What they *didn't* know was that Applebaum felt left out most of the time. He was embarrassed that he couldn't do anything. When his mother asked him why he didn't have some friends over to play, he wanted to tell her that he didn't have any friends because he always messed things up and he was sure they wouldn't come even if he invited them. But what he said was that he liked being alone or, sometimes, that he had homework to do, or that he didn't like anyone enough to invite them over. Applebaum knew that when he told his mother things like that, he wasn't telling her the truth, but he didn't want her to worry about him or feel sorry for him. Now he was very excited about being on the team and having a bunch of kids to hang around with. He almost felt as if he belonged—at last! "I've got to hit. I've got to stop being afraid on the field," he told himself. But he wasn't at all sure he could.

The team spent most of the week before the first practice oiling their mitts with special oil that Cynthia's father had bought for them. Cynthia's father also invited them to come over while he burned their names on their mitts with a leather burning tool he had. When Applebaum had his done, it covered the whole back of the mitt. The final "M" was almost around to the front.

Cynthia's father seemed to think that Sophie was not the ideal coach for them, but Cynthia told him that Sophie knew as much about baseball as he did. "Maybe more," she said. "Besides," Cynthia told her father, "women can be just as good at coaching as men." Then she told her father to watch their team become the champions of the fifth grade league.

5

It rained during the night before the first practice, and when Applebaum arrived at the field, it was a mess of puddles. By the time everyone else arrived, the sun was trying to come out, and Sophie, in her rain slicker and carrying her clipboard, was putting the base bags around. Eleanor complained that they were all going to get very muddy. Sophie said that a little mud hadn't stopped Reggie Jackson, Babe Ruth, Jackie Robinson, Lou Gehrig, Yogi Berra, and all the other famous ballplayers who, even if they didn't play when it rained, at least practiced in the wet and mud.

The session was long—Sophie insisted that everyone have a chance at bat. She tried people

at two or three positions. Finding a place for Applebaum was no easy matter. Applebaum tried to keep his eyes on the ball when it was pitched to him or thrown toward him, but he always closed them at the last minute. He also put his arms protectively over his head when a ball came toward him in the field. Sophie tried to show him what he was doing wrong, just like Mr. Antonio, the gym teacher, and his father had done—but nothing worked. She was very careful not to give him more time than she gave to the other team members. At the end of

practice, Sophie herself took a bat and made a tremendous hit right over the heads of the out-fielders and into the weeds which covered the home-run area. Applebaum was as proud of her as he could be. "How could she be *my* grandmother? How come none of that talent came down to me? It must have stopped with my father and mother," he said to himself.

Later, over ice cream, Sophie told them they had the makings of a fine team. "Remember," she said, "courtesy and good manners are as important on the ballfield as home runs." Then she began to discuss how each position should be played. "The first baseman," she said, "must be . . . "

Eleanor interrupted to say that all morning Sophie and everybody else had been talking about "first baseman," "second baseman," "third baseman." Eleanor thought that they should all try to remember to say "first base-person" and so forth. Ernie said that would be quite a mouthful to say and that maybe they should say "first base-er." "At any rate," said Ernie, "I know what Eleanor is getting at, and maybe we should all try not to say 'first base-man' and the rest of it."

After talking about each position, Sophie said that before next practice, the team had to find a name to put on their T-shirts so they could have uniforms when the season began. She measured everyone's feet so that she could knit baseball socks. She said that she knew most of them could knit socks themselves, but she thought they had enough to do what with homework and baseball practice. After some discussion, they decided that red would be a good color.

Then Applebaum spoke up. "Uh," said Applebaum while the rest of them waited, "why not call ourselves The Purls?" He explained that it would be appropriate to name themselves after a knitting stitch since it was knitting that had made them famous in fourth grade and since Sophie's store was their sponsor. Frankie whispered to Alfred that Applebaum had just said the longest sentence of his life!

"What a marvelous idea," said Sophie. Then she suggested that gray with red letters would make handsome T-shirts. Frankie said that maybe they could have crossed knitting needles as their emblem. After he said it, he laughed so hard that he fell on the floor. But the others thought it was a good idea. Sophie said she would ask a friend of hers who manufactured emblems to sew on clothing and hats if he could design an emblem with crossed needles for them. The emblem would be on their T-shirts under THE PURLS. Sophie's name would be on the back. There would be an emblem patch to sew on their baseball caps.

By the time they left the ice cream store, the sun was shining brightly and everyone went home tired and happy to wash the mud off and throw their practice clothes in the wash. Applebaum's father asked him how practice was going and if his grandmother was helping him. He complained that whenever Sophie came to dinner, she refused to talk about the team. "In fact, she told me that what happened with you was just between the two of you, and if I wanted to know anything, I should come to the games and see for myself." Then he asked if Applebaum had gotten a hit. Applebaum hung his head and said no. He started to say he was trying very hard and enjoying it a lot, but by then his father had turned on his heels and walked away.

6

There were only two more weeks of practice before the first game. When the season began, each team would play seven games. If the team won, it would get two points; if it tied (there were no extra innings played in the fifth grade league), each team would get one point. If the team lost, it got no points at all. At the end of the season, the teams with the most points played each other for the championship.

Sophie began each practice with warm-up exercises. Applebaum's physical condition was improving even though his game was not. He could run fast without huffing and puffing and already his muscles were bigger and harder.

Sophie led the team through a program of toe touches, toe grabs, jumping jacks, sit-ups, hurdle stretches, and elbow-to-knee bends. She was always ready for more even though the team was red-faced and sweaty. Sophie herself

pitched and hit grounders and fly balls into the field and to each base while the players tried out at different positions. She watched very carefully to see who were the smartest and fastest runners, the best fielders, the most powerful batters. During running practice, Applebaum surprised everyone by being one of the fastest runners, but he wasn't one of the smartest. He never remembered which way to run or when to run. Everyone got a chance to bat and to play a couple of positions. No matter how much Sophie coached, Applebaum never hit the ball. During a break, while the team had some juice, Sophie would lead a discussion during which she told people what they could do better. She even showed them how and watched and corrected while they did it.

In spite of the time Sophie took with him, and in spite of his strong muscles, Applebaum still couldn't hit the ball or catch it. One day Sophie sat down with Applebaum alone and told him that being shrewd and trying to out-think your opponent and taking time to size up situations were as important as hitting home runs—although that was very important too. "But, Stanley," she said, "if you don't get on base, nothing else matters." Then she continued with the team practice, working on the best and safest way to slide.

Sophie drew up the starting lineup and assigned positions for the first game on the last practice day. Cynthia, who was quick and smart and good at recovering grounders, was the shortstop. Eleanor and Arthur would alternate pitching duties. Ernie was catcher. Frankie, who had a strong arm and was a smart runner, was to play third base. Philip was put at second base. Alfred, who was fast and good at catching, was the center fielder. Because Edward was left-handed, he was assigned to first base. Richard's spectacular throwing arm meant he was a natural for left field. That left Applebaum. He waited to hear Sophie announce his position, but he knew that the only place left was right field. Sure enough, that's where Sophie put him.

The starting lineup for the first game was:

1. Philip
2. Edward
3. Cynthia
4. Frankie
5. Richard
6. Alfred
7. Ernie
8. Eleanor (Arthur)
9. Applebaum

At the last practice before the first game, Applebaum and the others got their uniforms. Sophie gave each team member a pair of baseball socks which were bright red and to be worn over regular socks. She distributed the T-shirts with the crossed needles and THE PURLS in big letters on the front and SOPHIE'S PLACE on the back. The baseball caps had a fancy emblem on the front with the same crossed needles with SP superimposed over them. The regulation equipment was from the school's supply: catcher's mask and chest protector, hard hats, and bats. When Applebaum tried on his uniform, he felt

good. With their uniforms on, The Purls suddenly changed from just a bunch of kids into a real team. Applebaum was proud to be part of it.

Ernie told the team that Buster, his dog, had offered to be the team mascot—to bring them good luck. Frankie said that Buster might run out on the field and break up the game, but Ernie assured him that Buster knew enough to sit quietly and sleep while all the excitement was going on. Eleanor said she would feel great knowing Buster was with them bringing all that good luck. Applebaum wished he had a pet like

Buster, but his mother had allergies. All he had was a couple of goldfish. He could hardly bring his goldfish with him to a baseball game, he thought.

In spite of his uniform and the team spirit, Applebaum still didn't fit in. He rarely talked to anyone—even Sophie, his grandmother. He didn't even chew bubble gum when he was out in the field. When Eleanor asked why, Applebaum explained that his mother wouldn't let him because it might get stuck in his braces.

"There's a kind that doesn't do that," said Edward. "Maybe you should try and get some."

Alfred said, right in front of Applebaum, that everyone would be so busy watching Applebaum miss every ball that came near him in right field and let every ball go by him while he was up at bat that they wouldn't notice he wasn't chewing gum.

Ernie made Applebaum feel a little better when he complimented him on his new muscles, his running ability, and how hard he tried to do the right thing. Just then, Alfred stole Applebaum's new baseball cap from his head and ran away with it. But nobody followed him and soon Alfred came back and dropped the cap in the dust in front of Applebaum.

"Applebaum doesn't know which end is up," said Alfred. "Or which end is down, or which side is right, or which side is left, or anything." Cynthia said that maybe Applebaum would improve as the season went on. "We'll never win anything with him around," said Alfred. Ernie said that winning wasn't the thing. Learning to get along was what it was all about. Frankie wanted to know who was kidding whom? Of course winning was the thing. "People are always saying that winning isn't everything, but they know it really *is* and they just say that in case they lose." Applebaum looked dejected.

Sophie stood off to one side and listened. Then she walked over and said, "Let's hope we all do our best. That's all anyone can do. Now it's time to start practice."

7

The day of the first game finally arrived. It was cool and clear, just the right kind of day for a baseball game. Quite a crowd turned out to watch. Everyone's relatives and friends were there. Applebaum's parents came early so they could have good seats. Some of the opposing team's relatives and friends, and some members of the opposing team as well, called out nasty remarks about players who were sponsored by a knitting store and coached by a lady, but The Purls went about their business and warmed up. Edward's little brother was the bat boy and in charge of the cold drinks. Buster, Ernie's dog, was there to bring them good luck. He wore a red sweater, which Ernie had knitted for him the year before. On the sweater, Ernie's mother had sewn the team emblem.

Applebaum was nervous. There were little beads of sweat on his upper lip and he looked pale. The first inning, first Philip and Edward and then Cynthia struck out. The first two batters on the opposing team then struck out, one after the other. The third batter hit a grounder to Cynthia at shortstop. She scooped it up and whipped it over to Edward on first base for the third out. Applebaum stood in right field grateful that nothing had come his way. In the second inning, after one out, Frankie hit a double. Then Richard hit a slow roller to third and ran to first. Third base threw the ball to first base, but it went clear over her head and Frankie ran home from second base. Alfred struck out and then Ernie hit a line drive to second and the ball landed in the second base-er's glove and Ernie was out. The score at the end of the second inning, after the opposing team struck out three times in a row, due to some excellent pitching by Eleanor, was 1-0 in favor of The Purls.

The other team made two runs in the fourth inning when one player walked and the next batter hit an easy fly to right field. Applebaum shut his eyes and missed the ball altogether and let the runner on first and the batter score easily while the entire outfield looked for the ball that had gotten past him. The Purls managed to win the game 4–2 when Philip made it to second on a long fly to center field, which the other team's outfielder couldn't catch, Edward walked on balls, and Cynthia connected for what would have been a double but which turned into a home run because of errors. Whenever Applebaum was up at bat, he kept his bat on his shoulder. When Sophie asked him why he didn't try a little harder, Applebaum said that he couldn't tell whether the ball was going to be a good one to strike at or a bad one for a ball until it was too late.

Except for Applebaum the team began to work well together. Sophie was constantly at them to improve their skills, and after the games she got them all together and taught them new things. Sometimes she switched people around. But Applebaum never played anything but right field.

At the end of the season, The Purls had made it to the top of the league and the championship game.

8

The day of the championship game turned out to be rainy and the game was postponed. To Applebaum, the days before the rescheduled championship seemed endless. All he wanted to do was get the whole thing over with. Finally the day arrived.

It seemed as if everyone in town was there to watch, even the teachers from the two fifth grades that were battling it out. There were babies in carriages, old people with canes, store-keepers who had left someone else in charge, and the usual assortment of relatives and friends. Applebaum's mother and father came early, of course, and Ernie's dog, Buster, and Philip's cat with a red ribbon. "Absolutely everyone in town is going to watch me mess things up," thought Applebaum to himself.

The Purls warmed up first and then watched as The Alley Cats, the fifth grade sponsored by the bowling alley, warmed up. Coaches called last minute instructions. Umpires went out on the field. The ice cream man, whose truck was outside the fence, got down from his cab and came closer to watch. The Purls had done so well all season that nobody jeered at them anymore for being coached by the knitting lady or for being called The Purls or for having crossed knitting needles as their emblem. The game began.

When Applebaum described the game later to his aunt and uncle on the telephone (he hadn't asked them to come because he didn't want them to see him make a mess of things), and when it was reported in the newspaper, both Applebaum and the reporter said that it had been without a doubt the most remarkable and most exciting game they had ever seen. But at first it was boring.

One player after another either fouled out, struck out, or was tagged out. Inning after inning. People started to leave. Storekeepers started to return to their shops. The ice cream man started to get back into his cab.

Their last time in the field, the top of the seventh inning, The Purls made three easy outs. Nothing even came *near* Applebaum in right field. The players on both teams became more and more desperate and swung at everything that came their way when they were batting, except for Applebaum, who as usual did not swing at anything.

Suddenly Applebaum remembered. He would be the last at bat during the bottom of the seventh inning. "Only once more," thought Applebaum, "then the season will be over." He was glad he wouldn't have to play baseball anymore, but he was sorry he wouldn't have the team to hang around with and sorry his dream of being a star was ending so badly.

When The Purls came up to bat, the score was still 0-0. Ernie struck out. Eleanor almost walked because the pitcher was so nervous, but she hit the last pitch and popped a fly to second base. An easy catch. Two out. Then it was time for Applebaum to walk up to the plate.

Suddenly, in his mind he could hear everything Sophie had ever told him and see everything she had ever shown him. "This is it," he said to himself. "This is my last chance. I'll never in my whole life be proud of myself if I don't do something now." Applebaum walked to the batter's box very slowly. He wiped his hands with dirt before he gripped the bat. Very slowly he picked up the bat. Very slowly he took his stance at the plate. Very slowly he stood waiting for the first pitch. Before the ball left the pitcher's hand, Frankie turned in disgust and said to Ernie that the game might just as well be over. Applebaum, said Frankie, had never, in all the years he had known him— except that one time in second grade—ever hit a ball with a bat. Sure enough, Applebaum just stood there, his bat on his shoulder, not moving, as the first pitch whizzed past him. The umpire called a strike. Applebaum's teammates were picking up their gear and standing around getting ready to shake hands with their co-winners. They were only waiting for Applebaum to make the final out.

As the second pitch came over the plate, Applebaum stood there. Strike two! Then, when the third pitch came toward him, Applebaum closed his eyes and swung. He felt the ball connect with the bat. He heard it smack. He opened his eyes and saw the ball go straight down center field. He threw down his bat and began to run. Faster and faster Applebaum circled the bases. There was not a sound from the crowd. The Alley Cats' outfield stood watching Applebaum run while the ball lay on the ground not far from the center fielder. The Alley Cats' infielders seemed frozen in their places. There went Applebaum. From the batter's box to third base, to second base, to first base, and home. When he got there, Sophie, stunned, said calmly and quietly, "Now, Stanley, run back the way you came." Applebaum looked at her

briefly and began to run again. As he did, The Alley Cats pulled themselves together, and the crowd that was still there began to yell and scream. Applebaum ran from home, to first, to second, to third while The Alley Cats' center fielder threw the ball wildly to second base. The player on second base dropped the ball, picked it up, and started to throw it home when he noticed that Applebaum had made it home already.

A roar went up from the crowd. Hats were thrown in the air. Nobody picked Applebaum up and carried him around on their shoulders, but there was an awful lot of cheering, and his teammates shook his hand, slapped his back good-naturedly, and said, "Nice going!" and danced around him. Even the coach of The Alley Cats came over and said that he'd never seen anything like it and that Applebaum was some fast runner. When the umpire came over, he told them that even though the run didn't count, because a player must touch each base in sequence, Applebaum had been marvelous.

He'd never seen such great running. Then he declared the game a tie. Sophie gave Applebaum a hug and so did his mother. His father shook his hand and said, "I'm proud of you, Stan." Then his father stood by receiving congratulations from the spectators. The Purls got together in a circle with their arms around each other and gave a cheer first for The Alley Cats, and then for Sophie, and then for themselves, and then for Applebaum. After The Alley Cats had given their cheers, the teams shook hands with each other. Applebaum's mother and father invited both teams to have the victory barbecue in their backyard the following week. Cynthia's father told Sophie that Cynthia had been right—she was some fine coach! Then Cynthia's father and Ernie's mother said they were taking them all out for victory hamburgers that very evening. Sophie suggested that the grown-ups drive to the hamburger place and the teams get on their bikes and meet them there.

Applebaum's father stood there listening to

everybody making plans. He didn't say anything while all the talking and laughing was going on. He watched Applebaum's teammates slapping him on the back and saying nice things to him. He watched Buster, Ernie's dog, lick Applebaum's face while Philip's cat rubbed up against his legs and purred. He watched Applebaum who didn't seem to be as happy as everyone else. His face looked sad in spite of his smiles.

As the excitement died down, The Purls began to clean up the field and put all the bases and extra bats and other gear into Sophie's car so that she could return them to the school. The people began to leave the field and drive off in their cars and The Purls started to walk toward their bicycles.

When Applebaum's mother said to his father that it was time to get going, he said that she should go with Sophie and leave him and the car there. He wanted to talk with his son, he said, and they would be along in a little while.

Soon, nobody was left but Applebaum and his father. The sun began to go down and there were long shadows on the field. It was very quiet. Applebaum sat down on the bench looking glum. His father walked over to him and patted him on the back. "Good work, Stan," he said.

"I must be the dumbest person who ever lived. I ran backwards! I can't believe I did that," said Applebaum miserably.

Applebaum's father told him that going backwards had made history before. "Way back in 1938, when Grandma was a girl, a man named Douglas Corrigan thought he was flying an airplane from Long Island to California, but instead he went the wrong way, crossed the Atlantic Ocean, and ended up in Ireland. Everyone loved him because he cheered them up during a bad time just before World War II began." The history books mentioned the flight, his father told Applebaum, and called the pilot "Wrongway Corrigan" in a nice way because they liked him. "Maybe they'll call you 'Wrongway Applebaum,' " said his father with a smile.

"But once you told me about a football player

who lost the game for his team in the Rose Bowl a long time ago when he ran the wrong way," said Applebaum unhappily.

"Listen," his father said. "You are a *winning* wrongway person. You first ran the wrong way, then the right way, and you made a run even if it didn't count. And you ran like the wind, too. Also, you stuck out all the practices and worked very, very hard. I think you're terrific! I'm proud of you."

Applebaum said, "If the other team hadn't been so stunned, I never would have made it."

"That's true," said Applebaum's father. "But then, those are the breaks. Some people win and some people lose. You won, Stan. After all, you are probably the best runner in the class. Most people are best at something. They just have to try all kinds of things until they find out what they're best at. Like I said, sometimes we lose, and it's usually because somebody else's best is better than our best. And then we have to try harder." He stopped for a minute. Then he said, "Sometimes what we do best isn't what our family and our friends do best." Applebaum's father was silent for a long time. He looked as if he was thinking about what he had just said. "But, son, you are a winner."

Then Applebaum said he was afraid it would happen again and the next time he'd do some other dumb thing. "I'm always messing things up," he said. "I think I'll forget baseball altogether."

"Baseball isn't everything," said his father. "Maybe you should go out for track. In track," he explained, "they point you in the right direction and you just keep on going until you stop at the finish line. You never have to change directions, or make decisions where to go, and nobody throws balls at you, either." And then he added, gently, "But you don't have to do it if you don't want to, Stan."

Applebaum smiled at his father.

"You may be right," he said. "About track. It sounds like a good idea."

Then Applebaum picked up his glove and stood up. He and his father put the bicycle in the back of the car and drove away.